BOYZ RULE!

Bull Riding

Felice Arena and Phil Kettle

illustrated by
David Cox

First published 2003 by
MACMILLAN EDUCATION AUSTRALIA PTY LTD
627 Chapel Street, South Yarra, Australia 3141

This edition first published in the United States of America
in 2004 by MONDO Publishing.

For information contact:
MONDO Publishing
980 Avenue of the Americas
New York, NY 10018

Visit our web site at http://www.mondopub.com

04 05 06 07 08 09   9 8 7 6 5 4 3 2 1

ISBN 1-59336-370-2 (PB)

Library of Congress Cataloging-in-Publication Data

Arena, Felice, 1968-
    Bull riding / Felice Arena and Phil Kettle ; illustrated by David Cox.
    p. cm. -- (Boyz rule!)
    Summary: Con and Josh visit the farm of Josh's uncle and dream of riding
    bulls. Includes related miscellanea as well as questions to test the reader's
    comprehension.
    ISBN: 1-59336-370-2 (pbk.)
    [1. Farms--Fiction. 2. Cowboys--Fiction.] I. Kettle, Phil, 1955- II. Cox, David,
    1933 - ill. III. Title.

PZ7.A6825Bu 2004
[E]--dc22

                                                                    2004045807

Project Management by Limelight Press Pty Ltd
Cover and text design by Lore Foye
Illustrations by David Cox

Printed in Hong Kong

Contents

Josh   Con

CHAPTER 1

Howdy Cowboy

Best friends Josh and Con have
been invited to spend the weekend
at Josh's uncle's farm. The farm has
lots of animals, including two calves
in one of the paddocks. The boys
finish their lunch and decide to
explore the farm. Josh's auntie gives
each of them a cowboy hat to wear.

Josh "I really feel like a cowboy with this hat on."

Con "Well, I've never seen a cowboy wearing shorts."

Josh "This cowboy does."

Con "So, what do cowboys do on their farms?"

Josh bends over and picks up a piece of straw from the ground and puts it in the corner of his mouth.

Josh "They chew a lot of straw, then spit on the ground."

Con "That sounds cool. Bet I can spit farther than you can."

Josh "No way, I bet I can spit over that fence."

Josh points to the fence in front of them.

Con heads over there and does a big suck-back then spits. A big loogie smacks onto the top rail of the fence.

Josh "I told you you couldn't do it."
Con "Well, Hot Shot, let's see how good you are."

Josh does a big suck-back and then spits, but the spit only just makes it out of his mouth. It dribbles down his chin and lands on his shoe.

Con "Yeah, you're really good. So, what else do cowboys do other than chew straw and spit?"

Josh "They ride around on horses and round up cows."

Con "Have you ever ridden a horse?"

Josh "No, but I bet I'd be really good at it."

Con "You think you're good at everything you do."

Josh "No, I don't. It's just that I know I'm better at most things than you are."

Con "Yeah, right. We should find a horse and see who's the best rider. We could ask your uncle if he has a horse we can ride."

The boys walk quickly back to the
farmhouse. Josh's uncle is sitting on
the veranda chewing a piece of straw.
They ask him if he has a horse they
could ride. Josh's uncle says that he
doesn't have a horse but he has two
calves he could round up and put in
the cattle yard for them.

Josh's uncle "You can try to ride them—you never know, you might both be born rodeo riders!"

CHAPTER 2

Are You Ready?

Josh's uncle has rounded up the
calves and they are now in the cattle
yard. Josh and Con sit on the top
rail of the fence looking at the calves.

Josh "Well, they *did* look like calves
when they were in the paddock,
but now they look really big."

Con "Yeah, I'm glad you're going to
go first."

Josh "Who says?"

Con "Well, you're the oldest and you
keep telling me you're the best, so
you better show me how it's done."

Josh "I'm only one week older than you but I actually think that you'd be a lot better at rodeo riding than me."

Con "What are you s'posed to say when you get on the back of a wild animal?"

Josh "I saw a movie once and the cowboy yelled 'Hi ho Silver!'"

Con "I thought they yelled 'Ride 'em cowboy!'"

Josh "Well, if I'm going first it means I'm a lot braver than you."

Con "Yup, guess so. But maybe you're also a little dumber than me!"

Josh points at the calf his uncle is now holding.

Josh "So, what's this, a boy or a girl calf?"

CHAPTER 3

Time to Ride

The boys stare at the calf, both
trying to come up with an answer.

Con "Oh, duh! It's easy to tell if it's
a girl calf or a boy calf—one is
called a cow and the other one is
called a bull."

Josh (pointing to a calf) "So, then what's this one?"

Con "I dunno. Maybe the girl calves should wear ribbons around their necks so you can tell the difference."

Josh's uncle tells the boys that the calf is a bull. He says that maybe they should spend more time on the farm as they still have a lot to learn.

Josh "Now that we know it's a bull, does that mean we're going to be great bull riders?"

Con "Well, I'm sure *I* will be."

Josh jumps off the rail and walks toward the calf, spitting the straw out of his mouth. He stands on a drum so that he can get onto the calf's back. Josh's uncle lets the calf go.

Con "Ride 'em cowboy!"

The calf just stands still, not moving at all. Josh looks disappointed. Con yells again.

Con "Hi ho Silver!"

Josh "This one must be a dud. It doesn't want to buck."

Just then the farm dog runs under the fence and barks at the calf. The calf starts to buck.

Josh "Wowee!!"

Con "Hold on, or you could be thrown over the fence!"

Josh "I'm too good. This calf will never be able to throw me off."

Just then the dog barks even
louder and the calf bucks even
harder. Josh, who has been holding
on really hard, loses control and flies
over the head of the calf.

CHAPTER 4

A Mucky Landing

Josh does a complete somersault
in the air before he lands, *splosh!*
in a really fresh cow pat. Con starts
to laugh.

Con "Great landing, champion bull rider!"

Josh "I've got poop all over me!"

Con "Well, you and your poop better stay away from me."

Josh "Except for the poop, that was really cool."

Con "Yeah, it looked really cool."

Josh "So now it's your turn."

Con "Well, it didn't look *that* cool."

Josh "Are you too scared to ride the calf?"

Con "No, course not."

Con slowly gets down from the top of the fence and walks over to where Josh's uncle is holding the other bull calf. Con stands on the drum and gets on. The calf is let free and this time it starts to run, jump, and buck.

Josh "You gotta hold on really tight."

Con "I am. I'm holding on so tight that I think my hands are gonna break."

Josh "Your calf isn't as wild as mine was."

Con "It's just that I can control mine better. So I *am* a better cowboy than you!"

Soon the calf comes to a complete
standstill and Con gets off. The calf
walks over to Con and puts its head
under his arm.

Con "This calf really likes me. He's not very wild at all."

Josh "No wonder he didn't buck you off—he's a wuss."

Josh and Con walk back to the
farmhouse.

Josh "Well I'm definitely a much
   better cowboy than you."
Con "Yeah, right. Who got thrown
   off and stinks of cow poop?"

Josh and Con both start to laugh.

Josh "Well, all I have to do now is chew on a piece of straw and learn to spit the right way."

Con "Yeah, that'll make you a real cowboy—not!"

Josh "I better take a shower before Mom gets here. She'll never let me in the car like this."

Con "I dunno. You're usually full of it anyway."

Josh

Bull Riding Lingo

Con

blooper A bull that does not buck very well.

kiss the bull When the cowboy's head hits the back of the bull's head.

lasso A rope with a loop at one end for catching calves.

out the back door When the rider is thrown over the back of the bull.

BOYZ RULE!

Bull Riding Musts

☞ Make sure that you wear a cowboy hat.

☞ Always chew on a piece of straw.

☞ Try not to step in any cow pats.

☞ If there are too many flies hanging around your face, stand in a cow pat. That will keep the flies away from your face.

☞ Make sure that you eat plenty of baked beans. Cowboys love them.

☞ Learn to ride on small horses first.

☞ Practice using your lasso on fence posts.

☞ Watch plenty of cowboy movies on television.

☞ Try learning to sing cowboy songs like "Home on the Range."

☞ Take your cowboy boots off before you go inside. Mothers don't like it when you walk across the floor with mud on your boots.

BOYZ RULE!

Bull Riding Instant Info

In 1883, Buffalo Bill Cody staged the first traveling cowboy show. It was called "The Wild West Show" and was a big hit.

"Rodeo" comes from the Spanish word *rodear*, which means "to surround."

Rodeos used to be called other names like "stampedes," "cowboy contests," and "roundups."

There are over 60 rodeo rules that make sure the animals are safe.

The goal of bull riding is to keep the bull between you and the ground.

A group of horses can be called a team, a harras, or a rag (for colts, or young males).

A group of cows can be called either a herd or a drove.

A cowboy who falls off a horse is called "sore." A cowboy who is thrown off a bull is called "very sore."

There are cowgirls too. Some famous cowgirls in history are Annie Oakley, Calamity Jane, and Belle Starr.

The most successful rodeo bull ever was named Red Rock. Red Rock threw off 312 riders between the years 1980 and 1988.

Think Tank

1 When Con and Josh first see Josh's uncle, what is he doing?

2 What causes Josh to fall off the calf he is riding?

3 What is "kissing the bull?"

4 What is it called when cowboys gather and compete at riding bulls and horses?

5 What is a lasso?

6 Why do cowboys wear spurs? Do you think it's good that they wear spurs?

7 Do you think the calves like being ridden by Con and Josh? What makes you think this?

8 Do you think Con and Josh are scared to get on the calves? Why do you think this?

Answers

1   He is sitting on the veranda chewing a piece of straw.

2   The dog barks, causing the calf to buck and Josh to fall off.

3   "Kissing the bull" is when the back of a bull's head hits the cowboy's face when the bull bucks.

4   The event is called a rodeo.

5   A lasso is a rope with a loop at the end of it. Cowboys use it to catch cows and horses.

6   Cowboys wear spurs to make their horse go faster.
    Answers will vary

7   Answers will vary.

8   Answers will vary, but Con and Josh seem to be scared to get on the calves because neither wants to go first.

How did you score?

- If you got most of the answers correct, you should consider being a full-time cowboy.

- If you got more than half of the answers correct, just make sure that the horse you ride doesn't buck very much.

- If you got less than half of the answers correct, forget riding horses, you should just walk!

Felice → ← Phil

Hi Guys!

We have lots of fun reading and want you to, too. We both believe that being a good reader is really important and so cool.

Try out our suggestions to help you have fun as you read.

At school, why don't you use "Bull Riding" as a play and you and your friends can be the actors. Set the scene for your play. You can't bring a bull into the classroom, so you'll just have to use your imagination to pretend that you are at a ranch and just about to ride a wild, bucking bull.

So...have you decided who is going to be Con and who is going to be Josh? Now, with your friends, read and act out our story in front of the class.

We have a lot of fun when we go to schools and read our stories. After we finish, the kids all clap really loudly. When you've finished your play your classmates will do the same. Just remember to look out the window—there might be a talent scout from a television station watching you!

Reading at home is really important and a lot of fun as well.

Take our books home and get someone in your family to read them with you. Maybe they can take on a part in the story.

Remember, reading is a whole lot of fun.

So, as the frog in the local pond would say, Read-it!

And remember, Boyz Rule!

Felice

When We Were Kids

Phil

Felice "Have you ever ridden a bull?"

Phil "No, but I have ridden a horse, a camel, and my dog."

Felice "It must have been a big dog."

Phil "It was a terrier. Actually it was a very flat terrier when I got off."

Felice "That's really cruel."

Phil "No, because I was only a baby and the dog was a stuffed toy."

Felice "So, do you think that you will ever ride a bull?"

Phil "Only if it was really tame."

BOYZ RULE!

What a Laugh!

Q How does a farmer count his cows?

A With a cowculator.